The first...of (a) stellar, long-running (military) romantic suspense series.

— THE NIGHT IS MINE, BOOKLIST, "THE 20 BEST ROMANTIC SUSPENSE NOVELS: MODERN MASTERPIECES"

I knew the books would be good, but I didn't realize how good.

— NIGHT STALKERS SERIES, KIRKUS REVIEWS

Buchman mixes adrenalin-spiking battles and brusque military jargon with a sensitive approach.

— PUBLISHERS WEEKLY

13 times "Top Pick of the Month"

— NIGHT OWL REVIEWS

I0533118

FLOWER OF DESTINY

A WHITE HOUSE PROTECTION FORCE ROMANCE STORY

M. L. BUCHMAN

Buchman Bookworks

Copyright 2020 Matthew Lieber Buchman

Published by Buchman Bookworks, Inc.

All rights reserved.

This book, or parts thereof, may not be reproduced in any form without permission from the author.

Receive a free book and discover more by this author at: www.mlbuchman.com

Cover images:

Labrador retriever © eriklam | DepositPhotos

Beautiful bouquet of bright wildflowers, isolated on white © belchonock | DepositPhotos

Brown Old Paper © gabyfotoart

Declaration of Independence on White House building © izanbar

French bulldog wearing police harness © lifeonwhite

Green grass background © halina_photo

SIGN UP FOR M. L. BUCHMAN'S NEWSLETTER TODAY

and receive:
Release News
Free Short Stories
a Free Book

Get your free book today. Do it now.
free-book.mlbuchman.com

Other works by M. L. Buchman: *(* - also in audio)*

Thrillers

Dead Chef
Swap Out!
One Chef!
Two Chef!

Miranda Chase
Drone*
Thunderbolt*
Condor*

Romantic Suspense

Delta Force
Target Engaged*
Heart Strike*
Wild Justice*
Midnight Trust*

Firehawks
MAIN FLIGHT
Pure Heat
Full Blaze
Hot Point*
Flash of Fire*
Wild Fire
SMOKEJUMPERS
Wildfire at Dawn*
Wildfire at Larch Creek*
Wildfire on the Skagit*

The Night Stalkers
MAIN FLIGHT
The Night Is Mine
I Own the Dawn
Wait Until Dark
Take Over at Midnight
Light Up the Night
Bring On the Dusk
By Break of Day

AND THE NAVY
Christmas at Steel Beach
Christmas at Peleliu Cove
WHITE HOUSE HOLIDAY
Daniel's Christmas*
Frank's Independence Day*
Peter's Christmas*
Zachary's Christmas*
Roy's Independence Day*
Damien's Christmas*
5E
Target of the Heart
Target Lock on Love
Target of Mine
Target of One's Own

Shadow Force: Psi
At the Slightest Sound*
At the Quietest Word*

White House Protection Force
Off the Leash*
On Your Mark*
In the Weeds*

Contemporary Romance

Eagle Cove
Return to Eagle Cove
Recipe for Eagle Cove
Longing for Eagle Cove
Keepsake for Eagle Cove

Henderson's Ranch
Nathan's Big Sky*
Big Sky, Loyal Heart*
Big Sky Dog Whisperer*

Love Abroad
Heart of the Cotswolds: England
Path of Love: Cinque Terre, Italy

Other works by M. L. Buchman:

Short Story Series by M. L. Buchman:

ABOUT THIS BOOK

Sergeant Nadia Bhatti and her Secret Service yellow Labrador Toni are always looking for trouble—it's their job. But they never expected to find it during a morning exercise run.

Director Herman Finegold of the National Herbarium seeks two things: an eastern wood-pewee bird sighting, and anything else to distract him from the terror of presenting a Memorial Day public lecture.

But when the dangers turn very real, can a historic flower save the day?

1

"I'M ON A QUEST."

Nadia Bhatti spun to face the voice. She would have leapt out of her skin if she hadn't been trained not to. When she stopped running, she'd been alone with her dog...or thought she was. Six a.m. Just past dawn in Washington, DC's National Arboretum was a splendidly quiet place to be. Typically

She made a quick sweep to make sure it wasn't a setup. Him, her, and Toni her yellow Labrador retriever.

By a trick of dawn light and tree shadow, the stranger had been hidden barely two meters from where she'd stopped. Something she absolutely shouldn't have missed.

No obvious weapons.

Hands in clear sight, both holding a book. For a moment she feared that she was about to be proselytized, then saw that it was a Sibley's birding guide. The last thing of importance was a set of binoculars hanging across his chest where she'd normally wear an FN P90 submachine gun. Part of the standard dress for a Secret Service officer.

He stood five-seven, one-sixty, deep brown hair and eyes, a neat-trimmed beard and mustache. Lightly olive skin: Arabic or Jewish, probably the latter. Good-looking without being especially handsome. Her training had her automatically noting the ten other common features that a sketch artist might ask if they had to profile him later. Overall face shape, nose, attachment of earlobes, eyebrows, and so on. His clothes were neat tan khakis, worn sneakers, and a t-shirt that proclaimed, "Come to the dark side, we have cookies."

"I spoke because I didn't want to startle you."

"Thanks."

"You didn't startle at all."

"I was trained not to." Then Nadia cursed. She tried not to let civilians know she was "other" except when she was on duty. She knew how to behave in her Secret Service gear, with she and Toni in their Kevlar vests, scouting whatever event venue needed to be checked for bombs. Dressed as herself, she never knew how to behave.

She eased back off full alert and continued with the reason she'd stopped...while keeping an eye on the interloper. Who actually still hadn't moved, making *her* the interloper on *his* morning bird watch.

It was already over ninety degrees—fast headed for another May record breaker. She ran a hand over Toni's flanks to make sure she wasn't overheating. Nadia had to keep a careful eye on her because, being a lab, she'd never complain until she collapsed with heatstroke.

Unlike her mother who'd been complaining on the phone this morning, "DC and I are having hot flashes. I can feel its pain." Then Mum had launched into far too much detail. "I'm going to die of heatstroke from within before I have a grandchild."

She had three from Nadia's sister, but Nadia had long since learned not to draw comparisons. Amara had made marrying well, baby making, and pleasing Mum into an embarrassing trifecta. Amara had always been the perfect daughter, making anything Nadia did automatically not good enough—such as joining the Secret Service rather than their family's top-rated food truck business. Of course, Amara's equally perfect husband, Avi, had turned out to be a chef *with* an MBA. He'd renamed them from Mumbai Delicacies to Food Truck India. "You must hit 'em between the eyes!" His favorite marketing statement.

He'd led them from two trucks to ten and was gearing up to take on Baltimore and Charlotte. It was a real pity she liked him, because it made it harder for Nadia to be angry at her sister for once again showing her up.

"Trained *not* to be startled," the stranger seemed to be tasting the words. "That's an interesting thing to practice. I mostly practice how to avoid people. I'm trying something new, my new quest: identifying bird sounds. Hear that?" He twisted left and pointed.

All she heard was a clutter of birdsong.

"*Pee-a'wee!* Bright and sharp. There! Again!" He seemed quite excited. Handing her his book, he swept up his binoculars and searched a nearby dogwood.

She checked him again. Had he intentionally filled

one of her hands in preparation for an attack? If so, Nadia could find no evidence of that.

The book still had a price tag on the cover. She opened it to a bookmark, and the binding crinkled.

"New to birding?" Why was she extending the conversation? Because her mother would have said it was only polite to do so.

Toni had laid down on the damp grass, but her head was still perky—not overtaxed at all. Though they needed to get moving before their muscles froze up. It was another kilometer back to the car and then a long day awaited them. Memorial Day was coming soon and that was a major event in the nation's capital, or rather a lot of major events. It meant the Secret Service would be at nearly the same level of duty as an inauguration. All of which required an immense amount of preparational work—her and Toni's specialty.

"I started this morning," the man continued staring through his binoculars at a tree less than five meters away where absolutely nothing moved. "It's tricky because this Chinese dogwood, *Cornus kousa,* has bloomed and it gives the bird many places to hide. But it definitely favors this tree."

It was indeed in full flower, sheets of white seemed to drape over the thick underlying green leaves.

"I'm Herman, by the way," he didn't turn from his inspection as he spoke. "Herman Finegold. It's spelled F-i-n-e, not F-e-i-n as you might expect, coming from the German. It was probably changed when the family came over in the 1800s. We landed in DC in 1870, escaping the Franco-German wars, and... I'm talking too much, aren't

I. Sorry, I do that when I'm nervous. I'm shutting up now."
He lowered the binoculars and hesitantly reached out to take his book.

Nadia passed it over. And wondered what to do with all his words or whether it was best to simply run away, as she'd been doing in the first place.

"You're very pretty," he didn't look up from flipping through his book, but instead hurried on as if he'd spoken only about the bird. He flipped some more pages, then turned the book and held it out for her to look at. "See? That's the eastern wood-pewee, *Contopus virens,* very easily mistaken for the western wood-pewee, *C. sordidulus,* except their call is quite different. *Tsee-tsee-tsee-peeer* in descending scale. For the western that is. It's their call, not the eastern's which is—"

She saw it! A small bird, that she'd have said was a slender swallow with a grayish chest, perched on the dogwood close behind Herman Finegold, spelled F-i-n-e, and released a loud *Pee-a'wee,* proving its species. Herman leapt in surprise and the bird fluttered away before he could turn. She caught the book before it could plop down onto the dewed grass, then handed it back to him.

"I missed it, didn't I?" He sounded so dejected that she didn't have the heart to laugh.

Then he laughed at himself and she liked him for it.

"That bird has been doing this to me all morning. I didn't think it was personal, but now you've proven the point. I think that's enough of that." He snapped the rubber cap on his binoculars.

2

AND MORE THAN ENOUGH OF SOUNDING LIKE AN IDIOT.

Thankfully, she'd missed his mumbled compliment. Though she really was remarkably striking. She had the breathtaking skin, dark eyes, and long ponytail of pitch-black hair that Indian women made look so effortless. Even without noting the athlete's body in sleek runner's clothes, she was enough to make him completely tongue-tied.

Clearly.

Talk about the wrong thing to say. Thing? *Things!* He was worse than a babbling brook once he got started. Was it any wonder that he did his best work alone in a basement? Maybe he could just tell the Arboretum director that he'd died, then he'd never have to emerge again.

"Why did you start bird watching this morning?" Even her voice was pleasantly melodic, the only hint her heritage had left on an otherwise local accent.

He uncapped and recapped the lens to keep his

hands busy. "I have to give a speech for work. I don't give speeches. Actually, it's worse than that. I have to give an entertaining hour-long lecture and I don't give lectures."

"Instead you mostly practice avoiding people."

She *had* been listening, which was a bad sign. He actually wasn't much used to that either. "Most people I speak with are botanical archivists like myself." Not beautiful women trained to not be startled.

He looked at her, down at her dog, then back up at her. No leash. Not only didn't they startle, the dog must be exceptionally well trained. It didn't take a genius, especially not in Washington, DC to understand what she was.

"You're Secret Service." Then he swallowed hard. "Was that okay to say aloud?" He looked around quickly, but all he could see was a pair of joggers just now coming into view from the dwarf conifer collection. Then he realized that she'd already been watching them. Even her dog's head was tracking them.

The silence between the three of them was unnatural until after the joggers passed. Was she about to do some crazy karate thing and throw him to the ground for speaking it aloud? They might be the same five-seven, but he had little doubt that she would make his demise appear both effortless and graceful.

"That's fine," her attention returned to him. "It's not a secret that we're Secret Service. Toni, that's with an I not a Y as she's a she not a he, and I, Nadia, also with an I not a Y because that's how Mum spelled it, are in the Uniformed Division. We dress much like any other policeperson when on duty. Except our vests say Secret

Service," she tapped the center of her chest which presently said Nike.

"Oh," he couldn't think up what else to say.

"Are you lecturing on birding?"

"No. I..." Herman sighed. He knew when he was hopelessly outclassed. "I'm just used to working with others like myself. Academics. Nerds. The Director of the National Arboretum wants me as Director of the Herbarium to give a talk to our major donors. I thought that trying birding might get me more used to... I don't know what I was thinking. Trying something new?" Like talking to a beautiful woman without sounding so much like...himself.

She smiled at him for a long moment, then held out her hand.

He shook it, surprised by both the strength of her hand and the calluses borne of using it.

"From one painful introvert to another, I wish you the best of luck." Then she snapped her fingers.

Toni sprang to her feet and they both ran off to the south and were soon out of sight around the curve toward the Asian garden collection.

He barely noticed when the eastern wood-pewee chirped at him from the *kousa*.

3

Nadia almost skipped her run the next day.

Captain Baxter was already turning up the heat on the dog teams even though Memorial Day was still a week away. For him, it wasn't just enough to check out an arena, hall, street, or whatever event area shortly before the crowds arrived. They had to be pre-checked until every dog and handler knew each twist and turn, and could find the exits blindfolded. She was surprised he didn't make them do it with both feet tied together. Or perhaps that was only in *advanced* site prep.

But she knew herself well enough to know that she shouldn't skip her morning routine. Running had always been her escape, her break from reality. She'd discovered track and field in high school. The more she trained, the less time she had to spend in the family business. Besides, she hated cooking.

Mum would always fuss and fuss, never satisfied.

Yet, the way the family told stories, it always sounded

as if her sister Amara had served her first three-course dinner while still in the womb.

Nadia had learned not only that training for races gave her an excuse to keep away. But if she won more, it led to higher-level competitions which stretched out the season. She'd eventually run right through All-state and Georgetown University Division I. She'd been scouted for the Olympics, but instead had run her way into the Secret Service. Within two years she'd had a dog, and certainly hadn't looked back to the food trucks she'd left behind—as much as possible—at fourteen.

With all of the pressure at work, their morning run was really the only time she and Toni had to themselves. So, they ran.

When she came up around the dwarf pine garden this time, she spotted Herman by his silhouette against the white-flowered dogwood. To his credit, he wasn't following her with his binoculars. In fact, as soon as he spotted her, he squatted down out of sight behind an azalea.

She eased to a walk and tapped a finger against the small of her back to make sure that her slimline Glock 48 was easily accessible.

He stood back up as she arrived.

"Hi," he held out a half-empty water bottle. She didn't take it. At his feet was a flexible dog bowl, filled with water. In his other hand he held a couple of dog biscuits.

It wasn't needed, but Nadia signaled Toni to stay close by her side rather than go to the water bowl.

Herman slowly lowered the water bottle. "What's wrong?"

"I don't know you," Nadia said it carefully, and kept her hand casually behind her back as if stretching, and less than two inches from her sidearm.

"But—"

"People attack Secret Service dogs."

"They do?" If he was an actor, he was a particularly good one. "I'm sorry. I just wanted to do something nice for you."

"Why? Because I'm 'very pretty'?"

"You heard that, didn't you? I was kind of hoping that you hadn't. Not that it's not true, it is. You're breathtaking. But I didn't mean for that to... Oh crap!"

"Why, Herman?"

"Because you were nice to me and I wanted to do something nice for you. Does that sound hopelessly lame?"

Nadia considered. It didn't. She held out her hand. He handed her the water and the dog biscuits.

The biscuits were Blue Wilderness Buffalo, about the most expensive and best brand around.

"Do you have a dog?"

"No. I bought them for Toni."

She sniffed the water.

"I just opened it."

She sniffed the biscuit, but didn't detect anything off. When she held them out to Toni, she looked at Nadia as if she was crazy. Toni had been trained to detect hundreds of different explosives from simple fertilizer-diesel combinations to highly elusive Semtex. Right, if they were poison, Toni might have no more idea than she would.

"*Gute Hund.*" Good Dog. And she handed over the treats, hoping that she wasn't making some awful mistake.

Toni crunched them happily. Then she looked up at Nadia, and Nadia pointed toward the bowl. Toni gladly drained it.

"*Ihr Hund spricht Deutsch?*"

"What?"

"Your dog speaks German?"

"Yes, but I don't. Except dog commands. I speak those. Except I should have understood that. *Spricht!* To Speak, is her command to bark."

Toni stopped in mid-lap of the water and barked sharply.

"*Gute Hund,*" she reassured Toni who'd been surprised at the command and was looking around for why she'd been asked to speak. She eyed Herman suspiciously.

Rather than risk speaking again herself, Nadia took a sip from the water bottle. Before she caught herself, she had drunk back half of what was left. When she tried to hand it back, he signaled for her to finish it.

"Uh, thanks."

Toni lay on the ground and, apparently detecting no threats, lay her head on her paws and went to sleep in that one-second on-off mode that she seemed to have.

Nadia returned the empty bottle after Herman retrieved the foldable silicone bowl. He slipped both into a small cloth bag.

"Sorry—" they both said at the same time.

"For what—" they stumbled over each other again.

Nadia held up her hands palm out and waited.

"I'm, uh, sorry that I didn't think about how careful you have to be to keep Toni safe. What were you going to say?"

Nadia couldn't help smiling, "I was going to say much the same. It felt weird not trusting your kindness. I'm sorry about that."

"I completely understand...now that I'm using more than two of my brain cells at a time."

"More than two? That's better than I'm doing this morning."

And it was his turn to smile at her.

"How's the presentation fear level going?"

"Oh, right on track. I've graphed it before, though for lesser events. I'm aiming for full-blown panic in just seven days—late Sunday night. By Monday morning when I start speaking, I'll be over that and into deeply resigned. The talk itself will be something of a blur, even though I love the topic. I'm told that I'm actually an 'okay' presenter, but I never seem that way to myself. 'Okay' is better than 'awful', isn't it?" He didn't wait for an answer. "I'll be so relieved by the end of the talk that I won't mind the kibitzing afterward. Then Monday evening, I'll feel an exhilarating false confidence that will last until the next time I'm asked to speak."

"You *actually* graphed it?" He said it so complacently. It was as if he wasn't fighting his weakness, he was embracing it.

He nodded happily.

"I wish I could do that."

"Graph my nervous collapse regarding a one-hour presentation?"

"No, what are you presenting on anyway?" Nadia checked her watch. It was still quite early. Unsure of why she was doing it, she stepped over Toni and sat on a nearby bench. Herman sat on the far end, but with one knee on the bench and an arm propped on the back so that he was mostly facing her.

Toni woke up and inspected her as if she'd lost her mind. She never just stopped in the middle of a run. In fact... Nadia tapped her stopwatch to stop the timer as it was rapidly ruining her average time, just as yesterday's stop had.

"The Identification and Preservation of Rare and Not-so-rare Flora. Sounds riveting, doesn't it? Actually it's a fascinating project. The Herbarium presently holds over eight-hundred-thousand specimens which...would bore the tears out of you."

"Eight— I can't even imagine a number that big."

"Just imagine a twenty-eight-story tall pile of one-dollar bills. Then, not only would you be rich, but you'd have a dollar for every specimen we've stored and cataloged."

She had to laugh.

"What?"

"Make sure that's in your talk. These are donors. Equating money to specimens like that might get them to dig deeper into their pockets." That was part of the food truck mantra—what can be added on as perceived value. Chicken biryani or, for just a few dollars more, the more authentic goat. Not quite implying that the chicken wasn't good enough, but that the discerning patron would prefer the more expensive item. Giving value, but at a cost. The fact that they bought goat for the same price as chicken was irrelevant.

"Oh, that's a clever idea. Maybe I should explain everything and you can help me figure out what to include?"

She glanced at her watch. Nadia had time, but not *that* kind of time.

"Right. Stupid. I didn't mean to imply— Shutting up again."

"No, it's not that..." Then she had an idea.

Tonight was one of Mum's family dinner nights. The trucks were all parked through Monday and Tuesday so that everyone could have a weekend off—though there were always some vats of this or that sauce bubbling away in the back kitchen for the next week's meals. Tuesdays was when all of the family gathered.

Mum had learned to stop inviting eligible bachelors, but she'd recently come up with a new plan. Now Nadia's various aunts and uncles would invite along one of their own children's "friends." All curiously male, Indian of course, single, and in their twenties.

"What time does the Herbarium close?"

"Five." Herman looked at her in some surprise.

For reasons unclear to her, Toni also woke up and looked at her with shock. Everything Nadia was doing lately seemed to be a surprise to Toni. As if she wasn't being herself. The question was, was that a good thing?

"I don't get off work until six."

"I'll be there!" Herman said a little too emphatically, but she'd already seen that's just the way he was.

Toni was still watching her as if she had been replaced by an alien. She stuck her tongue out at her dog who appeared to laugh at some silent joke. Or maybe she just yawned sarcastically.

"Great!" Nadia turned back to Herman. "Then you can give me a tour and I'll tell you what parts I find most interesting. If that will help?"

"Help? *Help?* That would be stupendously fantastic. I'll be waiting at the front door of the National Bonsai Museum. The Herbarium is mostly in the basement."

They shook on it, then she and Toni rose to finish their run.

It might be a little extreme, but it would at least get her away from another of Mum's candidates for courtship.

4

HERMAN LOOKED AT HIS WATCH.

Five thirty-seven.

Nadia had said she didn't get off work until six.

Yet, like some hopeless goon (hopeful goon?) he waited by the entrance to the closed museum.

Was he more excited by seeing Nadia again or having help with his talk? Why was such an attractive woman even speaking to him? Why wouldn't his brain ever shut up and just let him behave like a normal human being?

Sadly, he was used to this particular stream of internal chatter and had never found a way to tone it down. He had learned that others were *never* interested in it, which was fine. He didn't need to process *everything* out loud. He was comfortable with—no...resigned to?...his own thoughts. They were a familiar noisy terrain upon which he—

"Hi!"

He looked up and almost swallowed his tongue in

alarm. It was Nadia, he was sure of that. But she barely looked like herself. "You look...terrifying."

"Terrifying? I like that. Our final meeting today was just across the street with the DC Metro police. I hope it's okay that I just came over this way." She waved a hand at herself.

Black-leather shoes, black slacks, then, over a white dress shirt, a black bullet-proof vest that did indeed say "Secret Service Police" clearly across the front. A small machine gun of some sort hung across her abdomen. A wide leather belt held a sidearm, a radio, a Taser, and a baton dangled off a loop. She wore dark sunglasses that hid her lovely eyes.

Toni was now on a leash, that attached to a bullet-proof vest of her own that also declared "Police."

He held up his hands and protested, "I'm innocent. Honest. I'm just a flora archivist."

"I don't know," Nadia poked him in the center of the chest. "We have reports of a plant guy running around outside his area and spying on hapless birds." Then she grimaced. "Lower your hands, Herman, you're making me feel ridiculous."

"Ridiculous? Not a chance," though he did lower his hands. "Daunting. Magnificent. All powerful. You and Captain Marvel."

"Captain Marvel?"

He slapped a hand to his chest, suddenly aware of his palm placed directly over where she'd poked him. "You haven't seen *Captain Marvel*? The great blonde superhero who—"

Nadia swept her dark ponytail forward.

"Okay, maybe Wonder Woman."

"I didn't see that either."

Again he slapped his palm to his chest. "I'm aghast."

"I'm Nadia," she responded with a such a straight tone that he couldn't help but laugh. They shook hands solemnly as if meeting for the first time.

Curiously, in her running gear, she seemed a much more cautious and even dangerous woman. In her Secret Service uniform, looking like a one-woman army ready to take on the world, she was much less fearsome. Somehow, just a woman doing her job.

He held her hand for just an extra moment. It might have been too small a difference for any rational person to notice. But he was intensely aware of it as he led her inside, locked the door behind him, and they went downstairs.

In his tiny office, she stripped off her and Toni's vests. She dropped the big belt, but slipped the sidearm into the small of her back. She slung the machine gun over her shoulder so that only the strap showed. Again she was transformed. A beautiful women in business-casual dress, and the wide strap of the weapon might have been for a purse.

"You're not in any danger from me. And we're the only ones here."

"Sorry, I can't just leave these lying around." She shrugged an apology. "But Toni I can."

She pointed down to his office floor and snapped her fingers. Toni lay down.

Herman retrieved the dog biscuit bag from his desk

drawer and held it open for Nadia. She took two, then looked puzzled, before handing them back to him.

"It's not okay?"

Nadia was still frowning as she spoke slowly. "It's...not okay that *your* kindness should be presented as coming from *me*. You can feed those to her."

Herman knelt down and held them out tentatively.

Toni sniffed them carefully, then looked up at Nadia.

She whispered in German, "*In Ordnung.*" It's Okay.

Toni turned back, delicately collected them from his hand, and crunched happily on them for a moment before swallowing. Then she gave his fingers a gritty lick to clean off the last of the biscuit crumbs.

He pet her head. The fur on the dog's ears was so soft.

It left him wondering what Nadia's hair might feel like.

5

Naida's first impression of the herbarium was...unimpressive.

The National Arboretum's main floor had vast displays, the Bonsai Museum and the enclosed Tropical Conservatory. And outside were over four hundred acres of lovely gardens. She had to admit that she usually just ran through them, but they were gorgeous.

The basement herbarium was...in the basement. Concrete walls turned dark with age. Rows and rows of towering shelves were crammed uncomfortably close together. They were filled with banks of scuffed wooden shelves forming cubbyholes. Each was, in turn, crammed with thick papers.

"We house over eight-hundred thousand specimens in all major plant classifications. Oh, I already told you that. The number used to be much bigger but dropped drastically when we transferred our fungi to the US National Fungus Collection. They maintain over a million specimens. We also have one of the world's largest algae collection with—"

"Of fungus? Like the stuff between people's toes?"

Herman laughed, "That. And molds, yeasts—"

"Don't you have anything not...yucky?" She'd been intrigued by Herman Finegold. But a man who spent his days staring at microscopic infestations?

"Well, mushrooms aren't too yucky, are they? Truffles for shaving over wild boar pasta. Molds make bleu cheese blue. Or a wild mushroom-and-Swiss burger."

"Okay, I suppose those aren't *too* yucky." She realized how judgmental she must have sounded and tried to apologize with her tone.

"But we gave all that away. They're just so different. If anything, they're more animal than plant in how they access carbon for processing their..." Herman grimaced. "Okay, that's one of the uninteresting parts."

"I'm guessing that it's fascinating to a biologist, or an...animalologist, but I'm just a dog handler. How many in your audience on Monday will be ologists?"

"Not many." Herman sighed and leaned against a rack of shelves. "So what am I supposed to talk about?"

Nadia tried to think of how to help.

What could possibly be interesting about this place? Even if it was, how could she ever find it in this stark basement?

"Okay, Herman. Try this. Did you know that the Secret Service was founded three months after the Civil War ended in 1865 *to stop counterfeiting?* It had been a devastating war and almost everyone was broke, so counterfeiting was rampant. It is still the largest aspect of our operation. We didn't get into the 'protection racket' until after the assassination of President McKinley in 1901."

Herman walked slowly down the length of the row of shelves and back.

He did it again, all the while staring down at the concrete floor.

"I didn't mean to hurt you. I just—"

"No! No! Beginnings. That's great!" He grabbed her hand and dragged her down to another set of shelves that looked just like all of the others. "Do you know what this is?"

She just shook her head and wondered how soon she could politely escape. It would probably mean that she'd have to stop running through the Arboretum, which would be a pity.

"Originally conceived in 1828, it would require three different presidents and several changes in Congress to fund the United States Exploring Expedition. From 1838 to 1842, the seven ships of the United States Ex. Ex. sailed around the world collecting everything from penguins to plants to perch fish. They explored almost three hundred islands, performed the first major survey of the Oregon Territory, and returned with over sixty-thousand plant and animal specimens, many of which are in our Herbarium and the Natural History Museum. Hundreds of live plants are still in our Arboretum. This section, right here, was our founding collection."

He paused and looked at her.

Nadia nodded to encourage him. Because that was interesting, and she didn't even like history.

"Or this?" He again took her hand and dragged her to another area that looked no different than the first.

This time his energy was undeniable. When he didn't let go of her hand, she didn't mind. He squeezed it tightly as if trying to make sure she understood his excitement.

"In 1899, fifty years after the founding of the Arboretum, a railroad magnate by the name of Harriman was told that he had to take two months' vacation for the sake of his health. Being one of the richest men in America, he decided he wanted to hunt Alaskan bear. Along the way, he outfitted a ship, filled it with his family, servants, and thirty scientists, artists, writers, and Arctic experts. They returned with over *fifty-thousand* specimens and gave them to the Smithsonian. These," he waved a hand, "these are E. H. Harriman's actual plant collections and all of the botanical information his scientists collected while he mostly hunted."

He barely paused before turning to her in the narrow space.

"This, Nadia," he patted the shelves with his free hand. "This is history. History of plant life and the study of it. Here we've preserved exact pieces of our environment as it was in 1840, late in the Little Ice Age. Again in 1899 just twenty years after the invention of the lightbulb but well before the widespread use of electricity accelerated us out of the Industrial Revolution and into the Technologic one. These are the exact plants, with all of their DNA, atmospheric clues, and who-knows-what still intact. Here."

The excitement radiated off him. It was passionate and overwhelming. Some core of her being wanted to be a part of it.

Unable to even think about her feelings, all she could do was express them.

She kissed him.

After his initial surprise, he kissed her back soundly enough to, literally, make her toes curl.

Then the energy peaked and seemed to blow them apart until they were leaning with their backs on opposite sides of the aisle.

"That was...a surprise."

"It..." she laughed at such an understatement. "It was."

"Unexpected."

"Which is different than a surprise?"

"Um," Herman looked about him, then reached into a cubbyhole. From it he extracted a faded envelope. He slipped out a heavy piece of paper and turned it for her to see. It was a photograph of a small daisy, growing on a bit of dirt with a glacier poised to run it down.

"I feel bad for it. I always liked daisies."

Then he pulled out a cardboard packet. "I wish I could actually give this to you." He opened it up and turned it for her to see.

He held a daisy pressed between two sheets of glass. It was perfectly preserved from the top of its flower down to the fine tendrils of its roots.

When she looked up, she saw that Herman was watching her closely.

"It's the same flower?"

He gave an infinitesimal nod.

Their second kiss was as gentle as the first one was heated. Just the two of them, separated by two sheets of glass, and a flower.

6

IT WAS SEVERAL MORE MORNINGS AND NIGHTS BEFORE Nadia decided that she was going to sleep with Herman Finegold.

Each morning, he waited by their bench with water and dog treats. Each evening, he'd test another section of his lecture on her.

Yes, he was utterly exhausting to be around, but he was also inspiring. Where she was linear, probably why running fit her so well, Herman was constantly pursing shiny objects. She had to help him focus and refine his topics, but the give and take between them had an energy and excitement.

No matter how long the day had been, Nadia always looked forward to seeing him. The one night she'd had to cancel had made her feel awful. Far lower than made any sense.

She wasn't the only one. Toni always found the energy to do her yellow Lab bouncing about whenever they arrived at the Herbarium. And it wasn't just his insistence on providing the absolute best dog treats. He'd definitely won her dog's heart and he was fast on his way to winning hers.

On the Sunday night before his talk, Herman took her hand and led her out of the basement.

"Come on. We're going out to dinner."

"I'm not dressed for going out." She'd managed to lock her weapons in the gun safe in her car trunk, but was still in her work clothes.

They stood in the darkened Bonsai museum as he swung her into his arms. "You're too beautiful to not fit in anywhere. Besides, I'm not a fancy dinner kind of person. Are you a fancy dinner sort of person?"

Nadia could only shake her head. Toni tried to worm her way into the middle of the clench. Even a hand on her head didn't ease her back. When it came to sex, she was definitely going to lock Toni in a different room. Which left out her studio apartment. It was generous, but the only door led to the bathroom.

So far, they'd ordered in pizza or Chinese as he worked on his talk. She hadn't told Herman about her family's food truck business. Or anything about her family really. It was easier to pretend she didn't have an overbearing mother and a super-achiever sister and all the others up in her business than to explain them.

"Good, I'll take you to my favorite place to eat. Very casual, I promise. Besides, if I think any more about the talk, I'll totally screw it up. You've...we've...I've, no, we've made it way better than it ever would have been otherwise."

She'd been the one to reject any credit. It was *his* talk

and *his* sharp brain. She was an academic plodder at best. But he also made her feel like a really smart, happy plodder. It's like she was used to running and winning the race, but Herman had thought it up, made it fun, and gotten the whole thing organized.

He led her out through the bonsai trees and into the warm Washington, DC evening. The light was fading toward sunset, turning all of the monuments from shining white marble to a magnificent red gold.

"My favorite time of evening," Herman whispered.

"Mine, too," she whispered back because whispering seemed the thing to do.

Thank goodness for Toni. At the moment it felt as if the lab's leash wasn't for keeping Toni close by, but rather for anchoring Nadia to the earth. Maybe sensing her confused emotions, Toni stayed close enough that her own knee brushed against Toni's flank at each step.

Herman distracted her with bits and pieces of horticultural history as they progressed through a corner of the park and out the far side.

In fact, he distracted her so thoroughly that she didn't see where he was leading her until it was too late. She'd kept an eye on the flows of people, but not on—

"Nadia!" Her mother cried in joyous surprise.

Or perhaps it was shock. Nadia was probably the only person to use her brother-in-law's phone app to make sure that she *didn't* find one of the family trucks. Some parked in regular spots, but most of them roved to different neighborhoods each night and the app would tell you where. People came from all over for their Food Truck India fix.

Nadia was going to kill Herman for bringing her here. Actually, that seemed tactically foolish as she'd only this afternoon decided that she was going to sleep with Herman.

She could always just shoot herself.

No, that wouldn't work either. Who would take care of Toni?

7

"YOU KNOW EACH OTHER?" HERMAN LOOKED UP AT THE woman in the food truck.

The colorful sari was a distraction. But once he looked past it, he realized that he was looking at an older, nearly as lovely, version of Nadia.

"Your mother?" He asked it softly.

"My mother," she whispered back. She sounded as if he was talking about algae and fungi again. Dry.

Her mother waved them aboard. In moments, he was being introduced to an aunt and two cousins of Nadia. He'd told her all about his family and their small law firm in nearby Alexandria. It wasn't until this moment that he realized that he knew nothing about hers. Nadia must have done it on purpose? He wondered why. Then he wondered how much trouble he was in for having led her to her own family.

"Here, you two sit here." She escorted them to the driver and front passenger seats. "Tonight, I will serve you the best. The goat biryani is incredibly good. And the

chicken tikka masala. Yes, that will be good. Here. Here."
She served them each a tall iced tea.

Nadia looked as if she'd been frozen. Her face was
expressionless. It wasn't a look he was used to seeing on
her. The cautious runner—carefree only when she wasn't
aware of being watched. The fierce Secret Service agent
who had showed up that first evening. And the shy
woman who kissed like he didn't know what, but he
never wanted her to stop.

"Are you okay?" Herman kept his voice low.

"Of course, she's okay. Aren't you, my little Bebo?" Her
sharp-eared mother delivered a paper plate of samosas.
"Bay shrimp." And she was gone again.

"Bebo?" Herman tried not to laugh. If ever there was a
name that didn't fit this woman, her mother had found it.

"Death!" Nadia's eyes made it clear what would
happen if he ever used it again.

"Beer." He bit into the samosa and the flavor exploded
in his mouth.

"Food trucks can't serve alcohol in DC."

"No, Beer is my embarrassing nickname. My little
sister started it. Herman was too much for her as a kid.
My middle name is Lieber. The L was tough as well, so
she hit me with Beer and it stuck. Most of my family call
me that."

"Well, Bebo is off the table." Nadia's tone left no
doubt, but she relaxed enough to offer him a smile.

"How is that?" Nadia's mother delivered a plate of tofu
tikka skewers. "I'm Reena, since my daughter is too rude
to introduce us."

"I'm Herman. Finegold."

"Herman? What sort of name is Herman?"

"Jewish."

"Ah," and she was gone again. He could see her back at the order-taking station at this end of the truck, but she was clearly listening hard to them and barely paying attention to the customers.

"Should I make up a fantastic story when she—"

Reena swept back in and handed a plate of plain chicken stripped from the bone to Nadia. Nadia, in turn, set it in front of Toni where she'd curled up in the footwell—on his feet. His feet were far too hot and also going to sleep from the dog pressure. But it was hard to complain about the vote of confidence. He wanted to move their—his and Nadia's, not so much his and Toni's —relationship to the next level, but wasn't sure how to go about that.

He'd never met a woman like her. Or ever been as comfortable or fascinated by a woman. But how could she possibly think the same of him? He was a basement botanist archivist librarian with a particular penchant for cataloging historical expeditions that no one else ever cared about or—

"So, what do you do, Herman?"

He was impressed that he hadn't leapt right out of the seat. Maybe Nadia was rubbing off on him.

"Mum..." Nadia made it sound as if it was a good thing she didn't have her weapons with her. Though his hand had brushed over something at the small of her back when they'd embraced among the bonsai. Perhaps her mother should be careful.

"I—" And then he had a slightly wicked thought.

Normally he always responded with a full description of what he did—boring his audience to death by the second question, after his name. But in this case, "Your daughter has been tempting me to make a career change. The Secret Service sounds amazing, but I don't think I'd ever be brave enough for that. She's incredible."

Reena merely looked at him a little wildly before sweeping up their empty samosa plate and disappeared again.

Nadia looked at him sharply.

He shrugged. It was the best he had.

Nadia twisted around to watch her mother.

Herman glanced over his shoulder.

Reena was standing frozen in the middle of the busy cookline. Almost as frozen as her daughter had been when he'd accidentally dragged her to the wrong food truck.

8

"WHAT DID YOU DO TO HER?" NADIA WHISPERED.

"I lied. I feel kind of bad about that but I—"

She shushed him.

Mum turned, caught them watching, then hurried to help the next customer. There was quite a throng outside now. She didn't even say anything when she delivered the biryani and tikka masala.

"Oh, these are so good," Herman moaned. "No one cooks these like Food Truck India."

"Tell Mum that. Compliments about her food always make ground with her."

"Your Mum runs this truck?"

Nadia sighed. "Mum's the head chef. Mum and Dad own the rapidly expanding Food Truck India 'empire.' I'm the family failure."

"But—" Herman protested so suddenly that he choked on his goat. Once he'd sipped some iced tea and wiped a napkin over Toni's fur where he'd dribbled some sauce, he cleared his throat and tried again. "But you're a United States Secret Service officer. That's an *amazing* thing to be."

"So, you *do* want to join the Secret Service?" She tried to make it a joke but was too busy considering her own motivations. Nadia hadn't actually pursued the Service. They'd recruited her from university, and she'd liked the sound of it. Ended up really respecting the people they'd introduced her to, and she'd never looked back.

"Well, I would," he kept his tone light. "But it seems a coward's move just to avoid giving that speech for donors on Monday. Otherwise, a chance to meet women like you, I'm there in a heartbeat."

"Good thing you already met one." Nadia was feeling a little possessive about Herman Finegold at the moment.

"Sounds like a threat." Herman had a good ear. "But yes, I'd say it's a particularly good thing. Right up there with landing my job at the Herbarium."

"You're making my head spin, Beer."

"How about we go to my place and I try to make that really happen...Bebo?"

Nadia looked up to see Mum frozen in place between them, a plate of kaju barfi sweets. They were the most expensive dessert in the truck. Cut into diamonds, each cashew sweet bar was coated with a gloss of silver foil. In the last five minutes, Mum had apparently shifted from wanting Nadia to have an Indian husband to wanting her to have *any* husband.

Her mother was never slow to take advantage of a new situation. But apparently Herman's question was enough to really throw her for a loop.

Now it didn't matter if she did or didn't—she'd never hear the end of this.

9

SHE DID.

And felt wonderful!

Their taste in lovemaking had definitely matched. It was a quiet affair with gentle touches and soft whispers. And a great deal of simply holding each other because it just felt that wonderful.

Toni had slept right through it just past the foot of the bed. Nadia wasn't sure about trusting her own emotions at this point, so she appreciated Toni's tacit approval.

Her phone rang halfway through her morning run.

She'd left Herman asleep in his bed with a smile on his face. Which was fine, there was a smile on hers making her cheeks hurt. She'd left a note thanking him kindly and wishing him luck on his talk today and...then crumpled it up and threw it away.

She'd left another, much simpler: *Again. How soon?*

She yanked out the phone without slowing her pace.

"How soon?" Only as she spoke did she realize it could be her mother.

Toni twisted to see why she'd broken her stride.

"Where are you?" Captain Baxter.

Nadia almost plunged into a high hedge of boxwood in the world's largest boxwood collection (according to Herman).

Regrettably, her misstep slammed her into Toni. The two of them tumbled to the grass between two boxwood hedges. She managed to keep the phone to her ear.

Toni barked sharply as she leapt to her feet. She scanned the area, relaxed, then lay across Nadia's legs.

"I *was* running in the National Arboretum, Captain." One didn't waste Captain Baxter's time by hesitating or asking why he wanted to know. If she'd still been in bed with Herman, habit probably would have had her answering, "In bed with Herman Finegold, Captain." She was glad to not have to explain that one to the Captain.

If ever there was a singular alpha dog, it was Baxter. He ran the dog handlers of the Secret Service from his tiny office in the West Wing's basement with iron control and a decent amount of fairness.

"Good. Thought you might be. I hear Toni is with you. We have a threat." The captain had probably known exactly where she was based on a predictable average of her last hundred laps of the arboretum. He was scary that way.

"Where do you need me, sir?"

"According to the chatter intercepted by the intel guys, right where you are. Why would anyone threaten an attack on the National Arboretum?"

Nadia had no idea, so she kept her mouth shut.

"Find out what and where, Sergeant Bhatti."

She opened her mouth and closed it again when she couldn't find anything useful to say.

"What's your question?" He somehow heard what she hadn't asked.

Nadia tried again. "Sir. Did intel have any further information? The park has numerous buildings and is fairly large. I—"

"Four hundred and forty-six acres. I know. I'll try to send you some help, but they'll probably just be regular DC Metros, not the Service. It's Memorial Day. I'm spread from Arlington cemetery to the World War II Memorial. Sidekick has five events outside the White House." President Zachary Thomas was also a former Air Force captain and had a long record of refusing to hide merely because danger was a possibility.

"I'll just—"

Baxter's silence could stop a freight train.

"I'm on it, sir."

"Don't let me down." And he was gone.

10

HERMAN COULDN'T BELIEVE HE'D SLEPT THROUGH NADIA'S departure.

He also couldn't believe that she hadn't woken him up before going. Except she had, so he'd better start believing it.

The note had been a relief, stopping his self-doubt before it could truly take hold.

When he reached for his phone to call her and suggest that *How soon?* should be *Very soon!*, he was reminded that it was Monday.

Speech day.

Then he noticed the time, cursed, and dove for the shower.

He set speed records from his bed to his office that even The Flash would have envied.

Still, he was behind schedule.

He'd planned on an hour to review his notes and rehearse his talk one more time. Instead he had seven minutes. It was just long enough to realize that he hadn't charged his tablet computer, which was nearly dead.

By the time he'd transferred his notes to a charged tablet he'd found in someone's desk—he couldn't even remember whose it was in his current state—nine of his seven minutes were used up.

Again, standing in for The Flash, he raced upstairs and headed across the gardens. He'd never been a runner. Watching Nadia run, he understood that he never would be. She moved with a fluid grace even her dog couldn't match. Just thinking about that, and that she'd brought that same fluid grace to his bed, was more than sufficient distraction as he jogged across the grounds.

His plans for a leisurely walk gone, so was his time alone with the Capitol columns. The incongruity of the setting had always pleased his sense of aesthetics.

Twenty-four columns had supported the original East Portico of the Capitol Building. But when the Capitol had been expanded to accommodate a growing nation in 1863, and a far larger iron dome had replaced the lower wood and copper one, the portico had appeared overwhelmed. The unbalanced look had been resolved in 1960, but it had meant the removal of the massive columns. In 1984 they had finally found their place in the National Arboretum.

He'd always loved the setting.

Two columns had been broken, but the remaining twenty-two had been placed on a broad stone terrace atop a knoll at the garden's center. A fountain trickled down to a reflecting pool above the sweeping meadow. It was a pity that it was Memorial Day; in April, it had the best view of cherry blossoms outside the Tidal Basin.

Today Herman didn't like the setting so much. Because, as he hustled up Ellipse Road, the broad meadow allowed him a clear view of the people already gathering there.

He'd anticipated a dozen people...without really thinking about the National Arboretum's general popularity. His was also the first event of the day in all of DC, which meant that anyone who wanted to make a full day of the celebrations would start here.

There weren't a dozen. It looked as if there was a hundred or more.

"Oh no!"

Nadia had thrown him off schedule.

He'd scheduled (and graphed) his pre-talk, full-blown panic for Sunday night. *Last* night. Instead, he'd spent it with Nadia in his bed and had thought of nothing else except what a lucky bastard he was.

So now, rather than the scheduled utter resignation, the panic slammed into him hard enough to make him stumble on the wide curving border trail around the Ellipse. The Ellipse itself covered the east side of the columns' knoll. Nadia had insisted that he needed to appear calm—no matter how much he wasn't. Bluestar, *Amsonia hubrichtii*. Downy flox, *Phlox pilosa*. Little bluestem, *Schizachyrium scoparium*. Aster...but he was so rattled he couldn't even recall the Latin.

Just as he reached the top of the Ellipse, and could see the true scale of the crowd, a trio of black SUVs rolled up Ellipse Road and parked in the *middle* of the lane.

Secret Service men and women poured out of two of the vehicles. No dogs. None of them were Nadia.

Out of the third...

This just kept getting worse.

11

Nadia and Toni had scouted the outside of every building in the whole arboretum. After all, mining a tree with explosives, even one of the major trees in the park, wouldn't make much of an impression. On Memorial Day, it might not even make the news.

But all of the buildings were closed and sealed for the holiday.

Despite working far longer that she should ever have to in a single stretch, Toni had found nothing unwarranted.

She stopped and sat on a stone bench outside the Visitor's Center, popped out a bowl for Toni and filled it with water.

Toni drank, then flopped to the pavement. Not a good sign. They'd been pushing hard for two straight hours, and that was a long time for a dog to be on alert.

They might as well rest, because she couldn't think of where else to look for a bomb.

She glanced at her phone. Two messages from Mum,

no time for that now, no matter how angry the delay would make her. And none from Herman.

He should have called by now if he wanted to see her again. Maybe he didn't. One and done? Gods she hoped not. Last night, the whole last week had been simply amazing.

Maybe she should have woken him. She'd have still been in his bed when the Captain called, but it would have been worth it.

Herman had gone a long way toward convincing her that he was the best thing to happen to her in an awfully long time. But now her phone's silence was convincing her she'd managed to screw that up as well.

And she absolutely knew why. She'd hadn't even scrawled a "Good luck!" or a cheery "I'll be thinking of you!" across her note. It seemed that her mother was right and she'd never get married.

Nadia glanced at the oversized map mounted on the Visitor Center's outside wall.

Herman's talk would be starting shortly. Right in the center of the park at the Capitol columns. Unless she had some brilliant idea, she could walk over there and...

The Capitol columns.

They weren't a building.

But if most of the Arboretum's major donors were there...

Nadia was off the mark faster than her yellow Lab as they sprinted to the southeast.

12

HERMAN COULDN'T MAKE SENSE OF WHAT HE WAS SEEING. Not only was the crowd going to be standing room only, despite the Parks Department filling the whole courtyard with chairs, but the trio strolling toward him around the Ellipse made his throat go dry.

He knew that the First Lady Anne and her brother, Vice President Daniel Darlington III, were from a major Tennessee farm. The Darlington Farm was at the center of the Slow Food movement in the South and had become a major research center. Of course they'd be major donors, but he'd never thought about that before.

No sign of the President's limousine, so he was spared that, but the Darlingtons and the Second Lady were more than enough to turn him into a gibbering idiot.

"If you can talk to a woman as amazing as Nadia, Herman Finegold, you can talk to these people." He sounded less convincing to himself than he'd have liked. But he stepped forward to greet them.

13

NADIA SPOTTED THE BLACK SUITS AND TRADEMARK movements of the Protection Detail as they spread around the National Capitol Columns. Off to the side were three of the SUVs.

Things were definitely escalating.

A pair of them came off the northeast corner to intercept her path of approach. Not wanting to be shot, she slowed enough to identify herself.

Toni was panting hard, as was she. Not good.

The agents scanned her badge, then nodded. One circulated away, but a female agent remained at her side.

Her normal job was pre-event site safety. She actually had very little interaction with the protection details.

"What's up, sergeant?"

Nadia recognized the blonde agent from somewhere. She was hard to miss, bubbly, long blonde hair, and all the curves that Nadia had never developed herself... Detra Willand, the head of the First Lady's Protection Detail.

Not good had just become bad. Unbelievably bad.

"Intel of an attack somewhere in the Arboretum at an unspecified time today."

Detra glanced around. "Here?"

"Unknown. We've checked the perimeters of every building and walked most of the parking lots before I remembered that the only event in the Arboretum today is this one."

"We have to clear the site."

They were whispering as they came through the columns behind the podium and raised platform. Herman had already started his talk. In the very first row, close by the foot of the raised platform, sat the three members of the Executive Branch.

Some part of her registered a laugh from the crowd. Herman was doing well.

It was a relatively stark setting. Close-set paving stones formed a slightly irregular fifty by hundred-foot open area. Every ten feet around the perimeter stood a massive sandstone column. Each sat on a cubic plinth roughly four-feet high. The great round columns rose three stories to massive, ornately carved capital headpieces.

So, there wasn't much of anywhere to hide anything.

The chairs were just folding metal.

After talking it over, Herman had even decided against using a lectern of any sort. He simply had a stool for a bottle of water and his tablet. She could see that he was in the rhythm of his talk because, despite all of his initial fears and massive preparation, he wasn't looking at his tablet at all.

Which only left...

They'd paused at the rear edge of the platform. Toni sat abruptly and looked up at her.

Nadia knelt down to apologize to her dog for pushing her so hard, but then Toni looked at the platform again— under the platform.

The she whined.

Nadia squatted lower.

In the darkness, under the two-foot risers, something glinted.

The platform legs were painted dark, but something else was under there that wasn't.

She flicked on a flashlight and the first thing she spotted was a cell phone. With a wire coming out of it.

"Detra." Nadia had to grab the agent's arm and pull her down to squat beside her.

She didn't have to say a word. Detra unleashed a foul curse.

"If we try to clear the site, the triggerman could be anywhere in this twenty-acre meadow—or in the crowd if they're a suicider."

Detra nodded. "If we give any sign at all, they might trigger it. I'm surprised they haven't yet."

Nadia glanced over the edge of the platform, then pointed at the back of the crowd.

"Media," Detra agreed. Some poor stringer was going to get the story of their lives, if they survived. "They've got a van, so they might be doing a live stream. The triggerman wants to make sure there's some good footage first."

"How long?"

Detra shrugged. "Minutes?"

Which matched her own assessment.

Detra squeezed her arm. "I'll get as close as I can to the First Lady and the Second Family. Try to give me some warning if things go wrong."

Nadia nodded her agreement. They were already past making choices, and there wasn't time to second guess or even be afraid.

If anyone was going to disarm the bomb in time, it had to be her.

Detra rose slowly and strolled casually around the platform. Just another Secret Service agent circulating.

"*Blieb,*" Nadia ordered Toni to Stay. Nadia wanted to send her away, send her to safety. But couldn't think how to do it.

Instead, she called Baxter to connect her to the bomb squad, and crawled under the platform herself.

14

HERMAN REALLY WISHED NADIA WAS HERE TO SEE WHAT they'd created. The crowd was laughing at all the places they'd built in amusing moments. The First Lady had heckled him twice with charming but perceptive comments that had led him to explain an aspect of preservation that neither he nor Nadia had thought of.

He'd definitely have to get a tape of this from the TV guy in the back to show to her later.

A glance around showed that people weren't only standing along the columns, but even craning their necks around them to listen in. Out in the meadows, visitors to the arboretum were coming closer to see what was happening.

As he strode the stage, he spotted Toni directly behind him.

No sign of Nadia, but he couldn't imagine one being here without the other.

He started in on a story of the expedition in 2001 that had retraced Harriman's 1899 expedition. They had returned with a vastly different picture from the remote wilderness, and occasional devastation of the Yukon Gold Rush, that Harriman's team had witnessed and cataloged a century earlier.

As he described some of the changes that the Herbarium researchers were unraveling from those two sets of samples, one of his favorite projects, he glanced back again.

Toni was staring fixedly—under the back of the platform.

What could Nadia possibly be doing under there?

Then he felt a slight thump through the soles of his shoes. Too soft to be heard, but easily transmitted through the wood.

If she was under the platform, and thumping on something, that meant—

On the verge of shouting for everyone to run, he spotted the First Lady's protection agent.

She was looking straight at him.

Detra then made a patting motion with both hands, then flipped one in a circle telling him to keep going. She was standing very close to the First Lady. Two other agents stood just as near the Second Family. All three ready to...jump in front of the blast!

The only thing that Herman remembered from the rest of the talk was when Detra nodded happily and gave him a double thumbs-up.

He glanced behind him. Nadia now sat on the pavement behind the platform with an arm around Toni's neck. Her smile told him that everything was going to be alright.

15

SPRING HAD BEEN A LONG TIME COMING, BUT HERMAN HAD been right, it was worth the wait.

The cherry blossoms viewed from the National Capitol Columns were truly magnificent. It seemed as if the entire park was in bloom.

It might have looked odd, but she didn't care. In her white wedding gown, she and Toni had made a full patrol of the area just before the ceremony. Nothing blowing up today.

On that eventful Memorial Day, they'd even caught the triggerman. With guidance over the radio, she'd gotten the phone disconnected from the bomb.

Then she'd settled in to wait.

She'd banged her head hard against the underside of the platform when the phone buzzed sharply in her hand just moments later. She'd never told Herman that she could indeed be so startled, despite all of her training.

When the bomber made the call to trigger the bomb, the NSA had been waiting. They'd immediately traced the caller's location and Detra's people had taken him down hard with no one in the crowd any the wiser.

"We did good that day, girl," she told Toni in her best squeaky voice. Toni didn't seem to think that balanced out the white lace collar she'd been forced to wear for the ceremony. But her impatience was cured by a couple biscuits of her latest addiction, the Blue Wilderness treats that Herman had continued to spoil her with.

"Y'all sure did rock it," Detra agreed. "Almost as much as you're rocking that awesome gown. I've got to get me one of those someday."

"You'll need someone to go with it." Nadia looked down at her wedding bouquet. Herman had it made from the exact same genus and species of daisy that he'd shown her from the Harriman expedition. She'd definitely found the right man.

"Nah. Too much trouble. I just want the cool gown." And they shared a laugh together.

The two of them had become good friends over the last year; good enough for Detra to be her maid of honor. Detra had tried to recruit Nadia to the protection details, but she'd stuck with the Uniformed Division. She liked working mostly alone on the pre-event patrol too much to give it up. That was one battle she'd won.

"You're going to do even better today," Detra announced with easy confidence.

Nadia nodded. Much to her surprise, she was. Despite almost being blown up, Herman had shone that day...and every day since for her.

The music began.

Finegolds had streamed in from all over DC and

Maryland. And they'd held the wedding on a Monday so that all of her own family could attend *en masse*.

Yes, everything was perfect as she headed up the stairs from the reflecting pool to the fountain at the heart of the National Capitol Columns.

When she'd crested the last step, and could see past all of their friends and family, she spotted the one battle she'd lost.

Parked in a line at the base of the Ellipse, just waiting to serve up the wedding reception feast, stood a line of shining Food Truck India trucks.

OFF THE LEASH (EXCERPT)

IF YOU LIKED THIS, YOU'LL LOVE THE
WHITE HOUSE PROTECTION FORCE
NOVELS!

OFF THE LEASH

(EXCERPT)

"You're joking."

"Nope. That's his name. And he's yours now."

Sergeant Linda Hamlin wondered quite what it would take to wipe that smile off Lieutenant Jurgen's face. A 120mm round from an M1A1 Abrams Main Battle Tank came to mind.

The kennel master of the US Secret Service's Canine Team was clearly a misogynistic jerk from the top of his polished head to the bottoms of his equally polished boots. She wondered if the shoelaces were polished as well.

Then she looked over at the poor dog sitting hopefully on the concrete kennel floor. His stall had a dog bed three times his size and a water bowl deep enough for him to bathe in. No toys, because toys always came from the handler as a reward. He offered her a sad sigh and a liquid doggy gaze. The kennel even smelled wrong, more of sanitizer than dog. The walls seemed to echo with each bark down the long line of kennels housing the candidate hopefuls for the next addition to the Secret Service's team.

Thor—really?—was a brindle-colored mutt, part who-knew and part no-one-cared. He looked like a cross between an oversized, long-haired schnauzer and a dust mop that someone had spilled dark gray paint on. After mixing in streaks of tawny brown, they'd left one white paw just to make him all the more laughable.

And of course Lieutenant Jerk Jurgen would assign Thor to the first woman on the USSS K-9 team.

Unable to resist, she leaned over far enough to scruff the dog's ears. He was the physical opposite of the sleek and powerful Malinois MWDs—military war dogs—that she'd been handling for the 75th Rangers for the last five years. They twitched with eagerness and nerves. A good MWD was seventy pounds of pure drive—every damn second of the day. If the mild-mannered Thor weighed thirty pounds, she'd be surprised. And he looked like a little girl's best friend who should have a pink bow on his collar.

Jurgen was clearly ex-Marine and would have no respect for the Army. Of course, having been in the Army's Special Operations Forces, she knew better than to respect a Marine.

"We won't let any old swabbie bother us, will we?"

Jurgen snarled—definitely Marine Corps. Swabbie was slang for a Navy sailor and a Marine always took offense at being lumped in with them no matter how much they belonged. Of course the swabbies took offense at having the Marines lumped with *them*. Too bad there weren't any Navy around so that she could get two for the price of one. Jurgen wouldn't be her boss, so appeasing him wasn't high on her to-do list.

At least she wouldn't need any of the protective bite gear working with Thor. With his stature, he was an explosives detection dog without also being an attack one.

"Where was he trained?" She stood back up to face the beast.

"Private outfit in Montana—some place called Henderson's Ranch. Didn't make their MWD program," his scoff said exactly what he thought the likelihood of any dog outfit in Montana being worthwhile. "They wanted us to try the little runt out."

She'd never heard of a training program in Montana. MWDs all came out of Lackland Air Force Base training. The Secret Service mostly trained their own and they all came from Vohne Liche Kennels in Indiana. Unless... Special Operations Forces dogs were trained by private contractors. She'd worked beside a Delta Force dog for a single month—he'd been incredible.

"Is he trained in English or German?" Most American MWDs were trained in German so that there was no confusion in case a command word happened to be part of a spoken sentence. It also made it harder for any random person on the battlefield to shout something that would confuse the dog.

"German according to his paperwork, but he won't listen to me much in either language."

Might as well give the diminutive Thor a few basic tests. A snap of her fingers and a slap on her thigh had the dog dropping into a smart "heel" position. No need to call out *Fuss—by my foot.*

"*Pass auf!*" *Guard!* She made a pistol with her thumb and forefinger and aimed it at Jurgen as she grabbed her forearm with her other hand—the military hand sign for enemy.

The little dog snarled at Jurgen sharply enough to have him backing out of the kennel. "Goddamn it!"

———

Keep reading at fine retailers everywhere:
Off the Leash

ABOUT THE AUTHOR

USA Today and Amazon #1 Bestseller M. L. "Matt" Buchman started writing on a flight south from Japan to ride his bicycle across the Australian Outback. Just part of a solo around-the-world trip that ultimately launched his writing career.

From the very beginning, his powerful female heroines insisted on putting character first, *then* a great adventure. He's since written over 60 action-adventure thrillers and military romantic suspense novels. And just for the fun of it: 100 short stories, and a fast-growing pile of read-by-author audiobooks.

Booklist says: "3X Top 10 of the Year." PW says: "Tom Clancy fans open to a strong female lead will clamor for more." His fans say: "I want more now...of everything." That his characters are even more insistent than his fans is a hoot.

As a 30-year project manager with a geophysics degree who has designed and built houses, flown and jumped out of planes, and solo-sailed a 50' ketch, he is awed by what is possible. More at: www.mlbuchman.com.

Other works by M. L. Buchman: *(* - also in audio)*

Thrillers

Dead Chef
One Chef!
Two Chef!

Miranda Chase
Drone*
Thunderbolt*
Condor*
Ghostrider*

Romantic Suspense

Delta Force
Target Engaged*
Heart Strike*
Wild Justice*
Midnight Trust*

Firehawks
MAIN FLIGHT
Pure Heat
Full Blaze
Hot Point*
Flash of Fire*
Wild Fire
SMOKEJUMPERS
Wildfire at Dawn*
Wildfire at Larch Creek*
Wildfire on the Skagit*

The Night Stalkers
MAIN FLIGHT
The Night Is Mine
I Own the Dawn
Wait Until Dark
Take Over at Midnight
Light Up the Night
Bring On the Dusk
By Break of Day

AND THE NAVY
Christmas at Steel Beach
Christmas at Peleliu Cove
WHITE HOUSE HOLIDAY
Daniel's Christmas*
Frank's Independence Day*
Peter's Christmas*
Zachary's Christmas*
Roy's Independence Day*
Damien's Christmas*
5E
Target of the Heart
Target Lock on Love
Target of Mine
Target of One's Own

Shadow Force: Psi
At the Slightest Sound*
At the Quietest Word*

White House Protection Force
Off the Leash*
On Your Mark*
In the Weeds*

Contemporary Romance

Eagle Cove
Return to Eagle Cove
Recipe for Eagle Cove
Longing for Eagle Cove
Keepsake for Eagle Cove

Henderson's Ranch
Nathan's Big Sky*
Big Sky, Loyal Heart*
Big Sky Dog Whisperer*

Love Abroad
Heart of the Cotswolds: England
Path of Love: Cinque Terre, Italy

Other works by M. L. Buchman:

Contemporary Romance (cont)

Where Dreams
Where Dreams are Born
Where Dreams Reside
Where Dreams Are of Christmas
Where Dreams Unfold
Where Dreams Are Written

Science Fiction / Fantasy

Deities Anonymous
Cookbook from Hell: Reheated
Saviors 101

Single Titles
The Nara Reaction
Monk's Maze
the Me and Elsie Chronicles

Non-Fiction

Strategies for Success
Managing Your Inner Artist/Writer
Estate Planning for Authors
Character Voice

Short Story Series by M. L. Buchman:

Romantic Suspense

Delta Force
Delta Force

Firehawks
The Firehawks Lookouts
The Firehawks Hotshots
The Firebirds

The Night Stalkers
The Night Stalkers
The Night Stalkers 5E
The Night Stalkers CSAR
The Night Stalkers Wedding Stories

US Coast Guard
US Coast Guard

White House Protection Force
White House Protection Force

Contemporary Romance

Eagle Cove
Eagle Cove

Henderson's Ranch
Henderson's Ranch

Where Dreams
Where Dreams

Thrillers

Dead Chef
Dead Chef

Science Fiction / Fantasy

Deities Anonymous
Deities Anonymous

Other
The Future Night Stalkers
Single Titles

SIGN UP FOR M. L. BUCHMAN'S NEWSLETTER TODAY

and receive:
Release News
Free Short Stories
a Free Book

Get your free book today. Do it now.
free-book.mlbuchman.com

www.ingramcontent.com/pod-product-compliance
Lightning Source LLC
Chambersburg PA
CBHW020637130626
46552CB00003B/1282